WELSH CAKES
AND
CUSTARD

Cardiff Libraries
www.cardiff.gov.uk/libraries

Llyfrgelloedd Caerdydd
www.caerdydd.gov.uk/llyfrgelloedd

WELSH CAKES AND CUSTARD

WENDY WHITE

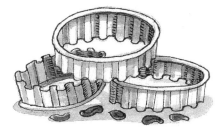

ILLUSTRATED BY
HELEN FLOOK

Pont

For Simon, Rebecca and Jonathan

First published in 2013 by Pont Books, an imprint of
Gomer Press, Llandysul, Ceredigion, SA44 4JL
www.gomer.co.uk

ISBN 978 1 84851 712 7

A CIP record for this title is available from the British Library.

This book is published with the financial support of the Welsh Books Council.

Printed and bound in Wales at Gomer Press, Llandysul, Ceredigion

Cawl and Custard
for Betsi Wyn

Betsi Wyn kissed Dad goodbye and ran to hug Mam-gu.

Betsi Wyn was excited. She was going to have dinner in school for the very first time.

'You're bright and early,' Mam-gu said. 'Have you had your breakfast?'

'I don't want any breakfast today,' said Betsi Wyn. 'I'm keeping a big space in my tummy for dinner.'

'You'll be hungry long before dinner time, *cariad*! You'd better have something to eat.'

But Betsi Wyn wouldn't eat a thing.

On the way to school, she hopped alongside Mam-gu. 'Can we run?' she said. 'I want to get to school fast.'

'You *are* excited, aren't you!' smiled Mam-gu.

All morning Betsi Wyn looked forward to her dinner.

While the teacher read a story, Betsi Wyn was dreaming about all the things she liked to eat.

When Miss Khan sent them out to play, Betsi Wyn was thinking about her pudding.

Yum, yum, yummy.

By the time they went back inside after play, Betsi Wyn's tummy was rumbling loudly.

'You sound hungry,' said Emyr Rhys as he and Betsi Wyn looked at a book together.

'I'm keeping a big space in my tummy,' said Betsi Wyn. 'There'll be lots of room in there for my dinner.'

'*Amser cinio*,' said Miss Khan at last. 'Time to tidy up and wash your hands.'

They all found a partner and lined up.

Betsi Wyn and Emyr Rhys held hands. They were very excited. 'I'm glad you're having school dinner,' he said.

Once everyone was ready, they set off for the dining hall. Betsi Wyn had been inside the hall lots of times before. That was where they went for assembly, when everyone sat quietly on the floor and sang songs. Betsi Wyn liked assembly.

When they reached the hall, Miss Khan opened the door to let them in. Betsi Wyn got a shock. The hall was full of big tables, and it was full of noise too! She held Emyr Rhys's hand tightly.

Miss Khan showed them where to sit. Then a smiling lady came over. She was carrying soup bowls. They were full of *cawl*.

'This is Mrs Philpot,' said Miss Khan. 'She'll be helping you every dinner time.'

Mrs Philpot put a bowl each in front of Betsi Wyn and Emyr Rhys.

'*Diolch*,' said Betsi Wyn politely. 'My favourite!
Cawl.'

'Just a minute,' said Mrs Philpot, picking up
an ice-cream scoop. Then she put a dollop of
cream-coloured splodge into Betsi Wyn's *cawl*.
Then she did the same thing for Emyr Rhys.

'Don't let it get cold,' said Mrs Philpot. 'You
don't have to wait for the others to sit down.'

Emyr Rhys picked up his spoon at once and
began to eat.

Betsi Wyn looked down at her bowl.

She liked the meat.

She liked the carrots.

She liked the leeks.

She even liked the parsnips.

But why had Mrs Philpot put . . . a great big
scoop of ice cream in her *cawl*?

Betsi Wyn looked around at everyone else.
All the other children were eating. They didn't
seem to mind having ice cream in their soup.

Betsi Wyn's tummy gave a loud rumble.

When Mrs Philpot came to collect the bowls, she was surprised to see that Betsi Wyn hadn't touched her food. 'Don't you like *cawl*?' she asked. 'Try a little bit. You'll be hungry later.'

But Betsi Wyn didn't want to try even a little bit.

'Never mind,' said Mrs Philpot as she took the bowl away. 'Perhaps you'll like your dessert.'

She brought them their pudding. 'Cook's best apple pie!' she said as she put down the dishes in front of them.

Betsi Wyn loved apple pie. Mam-gu made it for a special treat and it was Betsi Wyn's favourite pudding in all the world.

But when she looked in her bowl she got a nasty shock. Someone had poured thick yellow sauce all over her apple pie. Her pudding was covered in thick yellow gravy!

Betsi Wyn didn't like gravy.

She especially didn't like yellow gravy.

And she certainly didn't like it on her apple pie.

Betsi Wyn's tummy gave a sad, loud rumble.

'Oh dear,' said Mrs Philpot, when she collected the dirty dishes. 'Didn't you like your pudding either? You're going to be very hungry this afternoon. Never mind. It will be chips and yoghurt tomorrow. I expect you'll like that.'

'Yoghurt and chips?' thought Betsi Wyn. '*Ych a fi!*'

All afternoon her tummy rumbled and grumbled. She was glad when it was time to go home.

Betsi Wyn was quiet all the way to Mam-gu's.

'Did you like your dinner?' asked Mam-gu.

Betsi Wyn didn't say a word, but her tummy gave a loud, hungry rumble.

'Well,' said Mam-gu when they sat down for a glass of milk and a *cwtsh*, 'tell me what you had for dinner.'

'*Cawl*,' said Betsi Wyn.

'Oh, good,' said Mam-gu. 'You love *cawl*.'

Betsi Wyn pulled a face. 'It was horrible,' she said.

'Why?' asked Mam-gu. 'What was in it?'

'Meat and carrots,' Betsi Wyn began, 'leeks and parsnips and . . .' She stopped.

'Swede?' guessed Mam-gu.

Betsi Wyn shook her head.

'Cabbage?'

Betsi Wyn shook her head again.

'I give up,' said Mam-gu. 'What else was in your *cawl*?'

'Meat and carrots and leeks and parsnips and . . .' – Betsi Wyn looked at Mam-gu with wide eyes – 'and ice cream. All in the same bowl!'

'That was a funny dinner,' said Mam-gu. 'What did you have for pudding?'

'Apple pie . . .' said Betsi Wyn. 'Yuk!'

'But you love apple pie,' said Mam-gu.

'Apple pie with yellow gravy,' said Betsi Wyn.

'Oh dear,' said Mam-gu.

While Betsi Wyn watched her favourite DVD, Mam-gu got their food ready.

'What are we having for tea?' asked Betsi Wyn. Her tummy was still rumbling.

'Something a little bit different,' said Mam-gu. 'I'll need your help in a minute.'

Betsi Wyn was pleased. She loved helping in the kitchen.

Mam-gu tied the bow on Betsi Wyn's apron.

Then she showed Betsi Wyn a steaming saucepan, full of potatoes.

'You like boiled potatoes like these, don't you?' said Mam-gu. 'But now I'm going to show you a new trick.'

She helped Betsi Wyn put a big chunk of butter and a slosh of milk into the saucepan.

Then she showed her how to mash, mash, mash the potatoes until they were smooth and dollopy.

Betsi Wyn set the table while Mam-gu dished up their tea.

Cawl! Meat and carrots and leeks and parsnips.

And right in the middle was a big scoop of something soft and creamy.

'Taste it,' said Mam-gu.

Betsi Wyn shook her head.

'Go on,' said Mam-gu. 'You know what it is. You've just helped me make it.'

Betsi Wyn put a tiny bit on the tip of her spoon. Then she put it in her mouth. Very, very slowly.

'Mmm,' she said. 'It's yummy.'

'It's *stwnsh*,' said Mam-gu. 'Mashed potato.'

After Betsi Wyn had finished her *cawl* and *stwnsh*, Mam-gu took an apple pie out of the oven. 'Hooray!' shouted Betsi-Wyn.

Then Mam-gu went to the cupboard. She

came back with a brightly coloured tin. She showed Betsi Wyn how to spoon the powder from the tin into a jug. 'Not too much!' she said.

Then they put in some sugar and a little drop of milk. Betsi Wyn mixed it all together.

'I'd better do the next bit,' said Mam-gu. She warmed some milk on the stove and stirred it into the jug. Then she poured the mixture back in the saucepan. 'Can you find my special whisk, Betsi Wyn?'

Betsi Wyn found the whisk and gave it to Mam-gu. 'What are you going to do now?' she asked.

Mam-gu whisked the mixture gently on the stove.

Betsi Wyn climbed up on a stool to watch. 'It's changing colour,' she said. 'It's turning yellow!'

'And it's getting nice and thick,' said Mam-gu.

When it was ready, she spooned a dollop of the thick yellow sauce onto Betsi Wyn's apple pie.

Betsi Wyn put a tiny bit on the tip of her spoon. She put it in her mouth. Very, very slowly.

Then she grinned. 'It doesn't taste like gravy at all,' she said.

'That's because it's custard,' smiled Mam-gu.

When Betsi Wyn had finished her second bowl of apple pie with lots of custard, she helped Mam-gu tidy up.

'Did you enjoy your tea?' asked Mam-gu.

'Oh yes,' said Betsi Wyn. 'It was yummy.'

'I wonder what you'll have for dinner in school tomorrow?' said Mam-gu.

'I know already,' said Betsi Wyn. 'Mrs Philpot told me. Chips . . . with yoghurt!'

'Delicious!' said Mam-gu. 'Does Emyr Rhys like yoghurt?'

Betsi Wyn thought hard. 'I know he likes strawberry yoghurt,' she said. Then she looked up at Mam-gu with big eyes. 'But not on his chips!'

Good Job, Emyr Rhys

'What are you two going to do while we're out?' Nain asked, strapping Lowri Haf into her pushchair.

'We thought we'd do some cooking,' said Da-cu.

Nain frowned. 'You won't be making a mess again, will you?' she said. 'Like you did when you made pancakes!'

'Oh no,' said Da-cu. He winked at Emyr Rhys. 'That was just a little mistake.'

Emyr Rhys looked up at the brown, round mark on the ceiling above the cooker. 'We didn't know pancakes could fly so high, did we, Da-cu?'

Nain gave Da-cu a look. 'Just be careful,' she said. 'I don't want to come home and find mess all over the kitchen.'

When Nain and Lowri Haf had left for the shops, Emyr Rhys fetched Mwnci, Sam and Ted. He lined them up on the shelf above the kitchen worktop.

'There,' said Emyr Rhys, 'now you'll be able to watch.'

Emyr Rhys and Da-cu washed their hands then Da-cu got two aprons from the cupboard and tied one around Emyr Rhys.

'Right, chef,' said Da-cu, pulling on his own apron, 'you'd better tell them what we're cooking. Then I'll put the recipe where Mwnci, Sam and Ted can see it.'

Emyr Rhys looked at his audience.

Mwnci, Sam and Ted looked back.

'Today, I will be showing you how to make Welsh Cakes,' said Emyr Rhys. 'With the help of my assistant.'

EMYR RHYS'S WELSH CAKES

Welsh Cakes (*Pice ar y Maen*)

Ingredients
250g (or 10 tablespoons) self raising flour
100g (or 4 tablespoons) caster sugar
small pinch of salt
large pinch of mixed spice
half a teaspoon of baking powder
125g (or half a packet) butter in small pieces
75g (or 3 tablespoons) raisins
1 egg, beaten with a dessertspoon of milk

Method
1. Sieve together the flour, sugar, salt, mixed spice and baking powder into a large bowl.
2. Rub in the butter till the mixture looks like breadcrumbs.
3. Add the raisins.
4. Stir in the egg and milk mixture.
5. Mix with your hands to make a ball of dough.
6. Roll out the dough, not too thinly. Cut out about twenty circles.
7. Ask a grown-up helper to melt some butter in a heavy frying pan.
8. Ask your helper to cook the Welsh cakes over a medium heat for around 3 minutes on each side.
9. Remove the Welsh cakes carefully to a cooling rack.
10. When they are cool, sprinkle with sugar and enjoy.

Da-cu took a bow and lifted a big mixing bowl and a sieve from the high shelf. Then he found a tub of flour, a bag of sugar and a packet of raisins in the cupboard. Emyr Rhys got butter, an egg and a carton of milk from the fridge.

'What do we do first, chef?' Da-cu asked.

Emyr Rhys picked up the tub of flour. 'We measure out ten big spoons of this,' he said. And he put ten heaped spoonfuls of flour into a sieve over the bowl.

A little bit fell onto the worktop.

'Now we need a pinch of salt and a pinch of mixed spice,' said Emyr Rhys, rummaging in the cupboard. 'And half a teaspoon of baking powder.'

He measured them carefully and put them on top of the flour in the sieve. Then he held the sieve up high and shook it so the flour and salt, spices and baking powder got all mixed together as they fell into the bowl.

A floury cloud drifted over Mwnci, Sam and Ted and gave them a dusty white coat.

'Next ingredient?' asked Da-cu.

'Sugar,' said Emyr Rhys. 'Four big spoonfuls.'

And he counted four heaped spoonfuls into the bowl. Then he gave the mixture a big stir.

A little bit of sugar shook off the spoon onto the table.

'What's next, chef?' asked Da-cu.

'Butter,' said Emyr Rhys. 'Half a packet.'

Da-cu put the butter onto a plate and chopped, chopped, chopped it into little pieces.

'*Diolch*, Da-cu,' said Emyr Rhys. Then he tipped the butter into the bowl.

Some butter slipped off the plate and stuck to the cupboard door.

Emyr Rhys rubbed the butter into the flour and sugar with his fingertips. It took quite a long time. After a while he shook the bowl. Lumps of butter which had been hiding at the bottom jumped to the top. He rubbed those lumps into the flour too.

Some big bits of floury butter bounced out of the bowl and rolled across the kitchen floor.

'All right, chef,' said Da-cu, when the flour, sugar and butter mixture looked very crumbly. 'What now?'

'Three big spoonfuls of raisins,' said Emyr Rhys. And he put three spoonfuls into the bowl.

A few raisins rolled towards the sink.

'Well,' said Da-cu, looking into the big mixing bowl. 'We've got flour, sugar, butter and raisins. What do we add next?'

'An egg,' said Emyr Rhys.

Da-cu cracked the egg into a jug and whisked it with a fork.

'And now we need a little bit of milk,' said Emyr Rhys. He measured out a spoonful. Then he tipped the spoon into the jug and Da-cu mixed the milk with the egg.

Some milk dripped off the spoon and made a little puddle on the draining board.

'Shall we ask our audience what we do next?' said Da-cu. 'Ted, do you know?'

Da-cu waited for Ted to think of the answer.

'He says we should mix everything together,' said Da-cu at last.

'*Da iawn*, Ted,' said Emyr Rhys. 'That's exactly what we do next.' And he tipped the egg and milk from the jug into the big bowl. Then he used his hands to mix all the ingredients together and make a ball of dough.

Some bits of dough flew out of the bowl and landed on the dresser.

And on the plate rack. And on the saucepan stand.

'What do we do now, chef?' Da-cu asked.

'We roll it out,' said Emyr Rhys.

And he sprinkled flour all over the kitchen worktop. Quite a lot of flour fell onto the floor.

Then Emyr Rhys plopped the dough onto the worktop and began smoothing it out with a big wooden rolling pin.

The raisins were hard to flatten. One bounced out from under the rolling pin and landed on Ted's head.

Emyr Rhys took a round cutter and cut out lots of circles of dough. 'My assistant will now heat up the frying pan,' he said.

Da-cu lit the gas and melted some butter in a big, heavy frying pan.

Some of the butter slid onto the stove top.

Da-cu cooked the Welsh cakes in the pan, four at a time. When they were golden brown on one side Da-cu carefully turned them over.

Then he put them on a wire rack to cool a bit and Emyr Rhys sprinkled them with sugar.

They smelled delicious.

After Emyr Rhys had stacked the warm Welsh cakes on a big plate, he went to the sink to wash his hands. He ran the tap and looked out of the window at the front path.

'Nain's coming! Nain's coming!' he shouted.

Da-cu and Emyr Rhys looked around the kitchen. There was sugar on the table. There was butter on the door. There were eggshells on the worktop. There was flour on the floor.

'Da-cu, what shall we do?' said Emyr Rhys.

Da-cu grabbed some cloths. 'Start cleaning,' he said. 'Quick!'

They wiped the worktops. They wiped the door. They cleaned the table. They cleaned the floor. And they piled the dishes in the sink.

'Phew,' said Da-cu, as they heard Nain's key in the lock. 'We've done it. Good job, Emyr Rhys.'

'Well,' Nain said, carrying a sleepy Lowri Haf into the kitchen. 'Something smells nice.'

She looked at the plate stacked high with golden Welsh cakes.

'Those look delicious,' she said. 'You have been busy.' Nain put Lowri Haf to sit on the rug.

'Oh, my poor feet,' she said as she pulled out a chair. She brushed some floury bits from the seat and sat down.

'I've put the kettle on,' said Da-cu. 'Tea'll be ready in a minute.'

'You can be the first person to taste our Welsh cakes,' said Emyr Rhys, holding out the plate.

Mwnci, Sam and Ted watched.

'Lovely,' Nain sighed after she had had three Welsh cakes and two mugs of tea. 'These *pice ar y maen* are wonderful. Perhaps you could take some into school for Miss Khan on Monday?'

She put her mug down and looked up.

Emyr Rhys and Da-cu were smiling. Da-cu had butter on his cheek and flour on his chin.

Emyr Rhys had sugar on his nose and raisins in his hair.

Then Nain looked at the kitchen. There was Welsh cake mixture everywhere. She got up. 'I'm going to have a lie-down,' she said. 'All of a sudden I'm feeling very tired.'

She picked up Lowri Haf, went out of the kitchen and closed the door behind her.

'That was a close one,' said Da-cu. 'I think we got away with it though.'

'Yes,' said Emyr Rhys, shaking flour off Mwnci, Sam and Ted. 'Nain didn't notice a thing. What shall we cook next time, Da-cu?'

Da-cu opened the recipe book. He showed Emyr Rhys a picture. 'I like the look of this.'

'Oh, yes!' said Emyr Rhys. 'We could make it when Nain's at yoga tomorrow. What's it called, Da-cu?'

Da-cu put on his glasses. 'It's called,' he said, 'whipped chocolate mousse. That won't be messy to make. That won't be messy at all.'

A Star for
Saint David's Day

'*Hyfryd*, Emyr Rhys,' said Miss Khan. 'I love home-made Welsh cakes.' It was Monday morning and she was welcoming the children to the Sharing Corner.

'I've brought something to show you today,' said Miss Khan, holding up a photograph. 'It's a picture of me as a little girl. Can you see what I'm wearing?'

'A Welsh costume,' said Carys. 'That's what we wear on *Dydd Gŵyl Dewi*.'

'That's right,' Miss Khan said. 'It's Saint David's Day next Saturday and we're having a special concert in the Community Centre.

The whole school will be taking part and lots of grown-ups are coming. Our class is going to sing a song, the one we've been practising. Let's try it now, shall we? Everyone stand up.'

Then she went to the piano and started playing '*Mi Welais Jac y Do*'. It was a song they enjoyed singing. Everyone sang loudly and did all the actions.

'*Mi welais Jac y Do*

Yn eistedd ar ben to . . .'

They all pretended to be looking up to see the jackdaw sitting on the roof.

'*Het wen ar ei ben*

A dwy goes bren . . .'

They put their hands on their heads to point to Jac Do's white hat. Then they stood on tiptoe to make his bird's legs, all long and twiggy.

'*Ho, ho, ho, ho, ho, ho.*'

Everybody liked singing the laughing bit at the end.

Miss Khan smiled. 'That will be perfect,' she said. 'I wonder if anyone knows a song they would like to sing on their own.'

Betsi Wyn's hand shot up. 'I know a song about a lady who sells sweets,' she said. 'Mam-gu taught me the words.'

And Betsi Wyn stood at the front of the class and sang '*Hen Fenyw Fach Cydweli*' in a big, loud voice.

At the end everyone clapped. Betsi Wyn beamed.

'Well, Betsi Wyn,' Miss Khan said, 'would you like to sing that song at the Saint David's Day concert?'

'Yes please,' said Betsi Wyn.

That evening Mam-gu climbed up the big ladder into the loft. Betsi Wyn waited on the landing and practised her song. She could hear Mam-gu rummaging through boxes.

'Here it is,' Mam-gu shouted at last. 'Mammy's Welsh costume – all neat and tidy, just as I left it.'

In the bedroom, Mam-gu unpacked the box and helped Betsi Wyn get changed.

First she put on a red skirt and a white blouse.

Next Mam-gu tied a little white apron around Betsi Wyn's middle and put a shawl around her neck.

Then Betsi Wyn put on a white cotton cap and on top of that she put a tall black hat with white ribbons. Mam-gu made the ribbon into a bow under Betsi Wyn's chin.

'Oh, *cariad*, don't you look wonderful!' said Mam-gu.

Betsi Wyn looked at herself in the mirror. She loved the white apron and the little white cap. She loved the shawl and the big, tall hat. But the skirt was a bit scratchy.

'Don't worry,' said Mam-gu. 'For the concert you can wear white tights and then your skirt won't itch at all.'

Betsi Wyn couldn't wait for *Dydd Gŵyl Dewi* to arrive. She was very excited about singing her song. She practised it all day long.

She sang it as she played with Carys in the sand tray.

She sang it while she played at dressing up with Emyr Rhys in the *tŷ bach twt*.

She sang it as she played hopscotch with Emyr Rhys and Carys in the playground.

'*Hen fenyw fach Cydweli,*' she sang, as she hopped, hopped and skipped.

At last it was Saturday, the very first day in March.

That evening Mam-gu helped Betsi Wyn get dressed in her Welsh costume. Betsi Wyn was so excited she could hardly wriggle into her new white tights.

Last of all Mam-gu pinned a daffodil onto Betsi Wyn's shawl. Betsi Wyn bent down to smell it and the petals tickled her nose.

Then Mam-gu asked her to stand still while she took her photograph.

'How do I look?' Betsi-Wyn asked.

'Beautiful, *blodyn*,' Mam-gu smiled. 'As pretty as a daffodil.'

Mam-gu and Betsi Wyn were snug in their warm jackets as they walked to the Community Centre.

'Look, Betsi Wyn,' said Mam-gu. '*Seren wen.* Can you see that beautiful star?'

Betsi Wyn looked up. She could see a bright star, the one Mam-gu was pointing to, twinkling on its own.

She stared at the dark sky. The longer she stared, the more stars she could see.

'How many stars are there, Mam-gu?' Betsi Wyn asked.

'Hundreds,' said Mam-gu. 'Thousands.'

Betsi Wyn looked up at the stars again. 'Hundreds,' she said. 'Thousands.' Then she started to sing and her breath made swirly clouds in the cold air as she sang her song over and over again.

When they reached the Community Centre, Mam-gu helped Betsi Wyn out of her jacket. 'You'll be with Miss Khan until the concert starts. I'll sit in the hall and wait for Mammy and Daddy to come. They're finishing early in the shop today so they'll be here in plenty of time.'

Then Mam-gu gave Betsi Wyn a squeeze. 'Enjoy singing your song, *cariad*.'

It was noisy in the room behind the stage. The children were very excited. Betsi Wyn clapped and Carys skipped. Then they danced and danced and twirled. Twirling made their aprons fly out around them.

And all the time Betsi Wyn sang her song.

Then Emyr Rhys arrived. He was dressed in smart black trousers and a white shirt. He wore a checked waistcoat and a red bow tie and on his head he had a flat cap. Pinned to his waistcoat was a big leek. The green leaves at the top of it were all chewed.

He grinned at Betsi Wyn and Carys. 'Want a bite?' he asked.

Miss Khan clapped her hands. 'It's our turn next,' she said. 'Everyone line up in threes, just like we practised.'

Betsi Wyn found her place, in between Emyr Rhys and Carys. They held hands tightly. As they waited, Betsi Wyn practised her song.

'*Hen fenyw fach Cydweli*,' she sang.

Then Miss Khan said it was time to go.

The hall was full of people. Miss Khan told the children to go straight up onto the stage.

Betsi Wyn took her place with Carys on one side and Emyr Rhys on the other. Then Miss Khan started playing Betsi Wyn's song.

Betsi Wyn took a big breath and lifted her head up to sing.

But when she looked out from the stage all she could see were eyes, shining like stars in the dark. There were hundreds of them, thousands. And they were all looking at her.

Betsi Wyn opened her mouth to sing but no sound came out. She tried again but her voice had disappeared.

Her knees started to shake. She reached out one hand to Carys and the other to Emyr Rhys.

'Do you want us to help you?' whispered Carys.

'Yes,' Betsi Wyn whispered back. 'But you don't know the words.'

'Yes we do,' said Emyr Rhys. 'You've been singing them so much we know them all!'

Miss Khan started playing the introduction once again.

Betsi Wyn felt much braver with Emyr Rhys and Carys helping her. She looked out at the hall again. It didn't seem so dark now. There were lots of eyes looking at her, but they were all friendly.

There was Carys's mum and not far away was Emyr Rhys's dad.

Then Betsi Wyn spotted Mam-gu. And next to Mam-gu were Mammy and Daddy. They were all smiling up at her.

Suddenly Betsi Wyn's voice came back. She stood proudly and sang her song loudly, just as she had the week before in the Sharing Corner.

And just like the week before, everyone clapped when she finished.

So Betsi Wyn sang her song again, all by herself.

Then it was time for the whole class to sing their action song.

As they walked across the car park to go home, Daddy squeezed Betsi Wyn's hand. 'You sang really well, Betsi Wyn,' he said. 'We're so proud of you.'

Betsi Wyn grinned. 'Thank you,' she said. Then she pointed up at the sky. 'Look, Daddy, hundreds and thousands of stars.'

'Oh yes,' said Daddy. 'Hundreds and thousands.'

Mammy smiled, 'But none are quite as sparkly as our little star,' she said.

Mam-gu tickled Betsi Wyn under her chin. '*Seren wen*,' she laughed.

Then she started singing, '*Hen fenyw fach Cydweli . . .*'

And Mammy, Daddy and Betsi Wyn all sang along too.

BETSI WYN'S SONG

Hen Fenyw Fach Cydweli

Hen fenyw fach Cydweli
Yn gwerthu losin du,
Yn rhifo deg am ddime
Ond un ar ddeg i mi.
Dyma newydd gorau ddaeth i mi, i mi,
Dyma newydd gorau ddaeth i mi, i mi,
Oedd rhifo deg am ddime
Ond un ar ddeg i mi.
Ffa la la, ffa la la, ffa lala lala lala
Ffa la la, ffa la la, ffa lala lala lala.

The Little Old Woman from Kidwelly

A little old woman from Kidwelly
Was selling black sweets,
Counting ten for a ha'penny,
But eleven for me.
Well that's the best news I ever had,
Well that's the best news I ever had,
Counting ten for a ha'penny
But eleven for me.
Fa la la, fa la la, fa lala lala lala
Fa la la, fa la la, fa lala lala lala.

Traditional

41

Emyr Rhys
Takes a Bow

Emyr Rhys rushed out of school. He was carrying a big, bulgy bag and waving a piece of paper. He met Da-cu at the school gates.

'What have you got there?' Da-cu asked, as he gave Emyr Rhys a hug.

'A very important list,' said Emyr Rhys. 'It tells me how to do *dawns y glocsen*.'

'*Dawns y glocsen*?' asked Da-cu.

'Yes,' said Emyr Rhys, 'with Betsi Wyn at the school Eisteddfod.'

Emyr Rhys held up a shiny CD in a plastic case. 'This is the music,' he said. 'So I can practise.'

He shook the big bag. 'And these are my special dancing clothes,' he said. 'And my dancing clogs.'

Da-cu and Emyr Rhys started walking home.

'What about Betsi Wyn?' Da-cu asked. 'Is she going to practise the dance with you?'

'Oh no,' said Emyr Rhys. 'She's got her own CD. I'm going to be practising with you, Da-cu.'

'Oh,' said Da-cu. 'Now there's a treat.'

At home, Da-cu put on the kettle and poured a glass of milk for Emyr Rhys.

'No time for a cup of tea,' Emyr Rhys called. 'Come into the *lolfa*, Da-cu. We need to make a big space.'

Da-cu pushed all the living-room furniture back against the walls and Emyr Rhys rolled up the rug. Then Emyr Rhys pulled on his special black waistcoat and slipped his feet into the clogs. He tap-tapped his clogs on the wooden floor.

'This is great, Da-cu,' he said. 'It's just like the school stage.'

Da-cu put the CD into the player. He pressed the button and loud music filled the room.

Emyr Rhys picked up the list of dance steps. 'Here you are, Da-cu,' he said. 'This is for you.'

Da-cu sat down in his favourite squashy chair. He started to read aloud: 'Step to the right, tap-tap. Step to the left, tap-tap.'

'No, Da-cu,' said Emyr Rhys.

'What's wrong?' Da-cu asked.

'You need to dance too,' said Emyr Rhys.

'Oh,' said Da-cu. 'I forgot about that.' He stood up and went to stand next to Emyr Rhys.

'No, Da-cu,' said Emyr Rhys.

'What's wrong now?'

'You have to stand opposite me.'

'Oh,' said Da-cu. And he went to stand opposite Emyr Rhys.

Da-cu started to read the list again. 'Step to

the right, tap-tap. Step to the left, tap-tap.'
And he did the steps.

Emyr Rhys didn't move.

'Why aren't you dancing?' Da-cu asked.

Emyr Rhys looked hard at Da-cu. 'It's because,' he said, 'you don't look right, Da-cu.'

'Don't I?' said Da-cu. And he went off to look at himself in the big mirror over the fireplace. 'What's wrong with me?' he asked.

'The problem is,' said Emyr Rhys, 'you don't look like Betsi Wyn.'

'Oh,' said Da-cu. He thought for a minute. 'I can do something about that,' he said, and he pressed the button to stop the music.

Emyr Rhys heard Da-cu going out to the kitchen. When Da-cu came back he was wearing his big green gardening clogs and Nain's red apron.

'How's this?' said Da-cu. He did a little clog dance and finished with a twirl.

'Well, Da-cu,' said Emyr Rhys, 'you look a

bit better. I like your clogs and your apron. But Betsi Wyn has a frilly white cap.'

Da-cu thought hard. 'Back in a minute,' he said.

Emyr Rhys heard Da-cu going up and down the stairs. When he came back he was wearing Nain's frilly shower cap.

'How's this?' asked Da-cu.

'It's a bit flowery,' said Emyr Rhys. 'But it's all right.'

Da-cu pressed the button on the CD player and the music began again.

'Step to the right, tap-tap. Step to the left, tap-tap,' said Da-cu. He started to dance.

Emyr Rhys didn't move.

Da-cu stopped the music. 'I've got clogs and a red apron like Betsi Wyn,' he said. 'And I've got a frilly cap. So why aren't you dancing, Emyr Rhys?'

'Well, Da-cu,' said Emyr Rhys, 'you said step to the right, tap-tap.'

'I did,' said Da-cu. 'But you didn't move.'

'I know, Da-cu,' said Emyr Rhys sadly. 'It's because I don't know where the right is.'

'Oh,' said Da-cu. He thought for a minute. 'I can do something about that,' he said.

Emyr Rhys heard Da-cu going up and down the stairs. When he came back he was carrying Mwnci, Sam and Ted. He put them carefully on the floor.

'Now, Emyr Rhys,' said Da-cu, 'when I say "step to the right", take a step to Mwnci.' And he pointed to Mwnci on the floor.

'When I say "step to the left", take a step to Sam.' And Da-cu pointed to Sam.

'And when I say "step back", take a step to Ted.' And Da-cu pointed to Ted on the floor.

'Can you remember that, Emyr Rhys?' he asked.

Emyr Rhys smiled. 'Yes, Da-cu,' he said. 'That's easy.'

Da-cu started the music again.

'Step to the right, tap-tap,' said Da-cu, and Emyr Rhys took a step to Mwnci.

'Step to the left, tap-tap,' said Da-cu, and Emyr Rhys took a step to Sam.

'Step back,' said Da-cu, and Emyr Rhys took a step to Ted.

'*Da iawn*,' said Da-cu. 'That was great.'

Emyr Rhys smiled and took a bow.

'Thank you,' he said quickly, 'but keep going, Da-cu. Keep going!'

When Nain and Lowri Haf came home later that afternoon, Emyr Rhys and Da-cu were still dancing around and around the living room.

'Good gracious,' Nain said, as she looked at the furniture pushed back against the walls, 'what have you done to the *lolfa*?'

'And goodness me!' she said, looking at Da-cu in her red apron and frilly shower cap. 'What are you wearing? And why on earth,' she said, as she looked at the muddy footprints Da-cu's gardening clogs had made on the wooden

floor, 'have you brought so much mud into the house?'

'All in a good cause,' said Da-cu, and he went to the kitchen to fetch the dustpan and brush. 'You'll see tomorrow.'

Mr Evans, the head teacher, welcomed everyone to the Eisteddfod. Then Emyr Rhys and Betsi Wyn took their place on stage. They were very smart in their dancing outfits. Emyr Rhys looked out at the people in the hall. There was Nain with Lowri Haf on her lap. And next to them in the front row was Da-cu with a large bag near his feet. Emyr Rhys waved to them.

The music started and Betsi Wyn began to dance. She stepped and tap-tapped. Then she stepped, tapped and tap-tapped again. Emyr

Rhys looked down at his smart black clogs. He knew he should be dancing too. All the people in the hall were watching him. They were waiting for him to dance.

Emyr Rhys knew he should be stepping to the right and tap-tapping. But where was the right? Oh no! He couldn't remember.

'Emyr Rhys,' Da-cu whispered from the front row, 'what's wrong?'

'I can't do the dance, Da-cu,' Emyr Rhys whispered back. 'I can't remember where the right is.'

'Don't worry, Emyr Rhys,' Da-cu whispered. 'I can do something about that.'

Da-cu stood up. 'Wait a minute, everyone, please,' he said in a loud voice.

The music stopped and Da-cu sat down again. He rummaged in the bag near his feet and took out Mwnci, Sam and Ted. Da-cu sat them on his lap.

'Think about how we practised yesterday,'

Da-cu told Emyr Rhys, 'with Mwnci, Sam and Ted.'

Then Da-cu pulled something else out of the bag. He put it on his head. It was Nain's frilly shower cap.

Da-cu pointed at it. 'Remember this?'

Emyr Rhys looked at Da-cu wearing Nain's shower cap. He remembered Da-cu dancing in his green gardening clogs and twirling in Nain's red apron. He remembered Da-cu putting Mwnci, Sam and Ted on the *lolfa* floor. He remembered stepping to Mwnci, tap-tap, and stepping to Sam, tap, tap. And he remembered stepping back to Ted.

Suddenly he remembered which way was right. It was easy. The music began again and Emyr Rhys started to dance and tap-tap his clogs. He and Betsi Wyn danced and danced and danced to the music.

Da-cu beamed beneath Nain's frilly shower

cap while Emyr Rhys and Betsi Wyn finished their dance.

'*Da iawn,*' Da-cu called, as everyone in the hall clapped and Emyr Rhys and Betsi Wyn took a bow.

'*Diolch,*' Emyr Rhys called back and gave an enormous grin. 'Thank you, Mwnci, Sam and Ted.'

'And thank you, Nain!' laughed Da-cu, pointing to the shower cap on his head.

'Three cheers for Da-cu,' called Mr Evans the head teacher. 'Our Eisteddfod wouldn't have been the same without you. *Un, dau, tri*! Hip, hip, hooray!'

Pirates Ahoy!

Betsi Wyn held her party bag tightly and ran to Mam-gu. Mam-gu gave her a big hug.

'Well, Betsi Wyn,' Mam-gu said, 'what did you do at Carys's birthday party?'

Betsi Wyn thought hard. 'I didn't do anything much,' she said. She looked at Mam-gu. 'I was sad.'

Mam-gu squeezed her tight. 'Oh, *cariad*, why were you sad?' she asked.

'Because I wanted you to be there, Mam-gu,' said Betsi Wyn. 'I wanted you to be at Carys's birthday party too.' She sighed. 'I missed you, Mam-gu.'

'Well, you see, Betsi Wyn,' Mam-gu said, 'there wasn't room for everyone at Carys's party. But perhaps you should have taken a magic *sws* with you.'

'A magic *sws*?' Betsi Wyn said.

'A kiss,' said Mam-gu. 'Let me show you.'

She held Betsi Wyn's hand and said, 'Here's a magic kiss from me to you. It'll stay on your hand the whole day through.' Then Mam-gu kissed Betsi Wyn's hand right in the middle.

Betsi Wyn looked at her hand. 'I can't see anything.'

'That's because the kiss is magic,' said Mam-gu. 'You can't see it but that kiss is stuck tight to your hand. If ever you feel sad just remember the magic kiss and then you'll feel much better.'

They began to walk home. 'Mam-gu,' Betsi Wyn said after a few steps, 'will the kiss shake off when I wave goodbye?'

'Oh no, Betsi Wyn,' Mam-gu said, 'that kiss won't shake off. It's stuck tight.'

They walked a little bit further. 'Mam-gu,' said Betsi Wyn, 'will the kiss come off when I wash my hands?'

'No, Betsi Wyn,' Mam-gu said, 'magic kisses won't wash off.'

They crossed the road carefully and carried on down the street. 'Mam-gu,' said Betsi Wyn, 'will the magic kiss fall off when I go out to play?'

'Oh no, Betsi Wyn,' Mam-gu said, 'magic kisses don't fall off.'

They went past the little row of shops and the newsagent's. There was a notice in the window with a picture of a lost budgie.

'Mam-gu,' Betsi Wyn said, 'what if my magic kiss gets lost?'

'Oh no, Betsi Wyn,' Mam-gu said, 'magic kisses can't ever get lost.' And with that, she took her key from her bag. 'You know,' she said as she opened the front door, 'that magic kiss is stuck tight to your hand. If ever you feel a little bit sad just remember that *sws* and you'll feel fine again.'

Betsi Wyn smiled up at Mam-gu. 'Can I have a special magic kiss on Friday, before I go to Gwion's house?' she asked. 'He's having a pirate party.' Betsi Wyn looked down at her feet. 'The pirates might be scary,' she said.

Mam-gu laughed. 'I shouldn't think so,' she said. 'I bet you that the pirates at Gwion's party will be the friendliest pirates in Wales.

'But of course you can have a magic kiss, *cariad*, though you don't really need another one. The one I gave you will be there for always.' And she went into the kitchen to fill the kettle.

On Friday, Mam-gu helped Betsi Wyn get changed for Gwion's party. Betsi Wyn put on a stripy shirt and tucked her trousers into her socks. Then Mam-gu tied a spotty scarf around her head. 'There,' she said. 'You look just like a pirate, Betsi Wyn.'

As they were walking to Gwion's house, Betsi Wyn suddenly remembered something. 'Mam-gu,' she said. 'You've forgotten to give me my special magic kiss . . . in case the pirates are scary.'

Mam-gu smiled. 'You've still got the one I gave you after Carys's party,' she said. 'Magic kisses never come off.' But she took Betsi Wyn's hand anyway and kissed it. 'Here's a magic kiss from me to you. It'll stay on your hand the whole day through.'

'Another magic *sws*!' Betsi Wyn said. '*Diolch*, Mam-gu.'

Coming down the road, Betsi Wyn and Mam-gu saw Emyr Rhys and his grandfather. Betsi Wyn ran to catch up with Emyr Rhys as Mam-gu and Da-cu strolled behind them, chatting.

'Are you going to Gwion's pirate party, Emyr Rhys?' Betsi Wyn asked.

'Yes,' said Emyr Rhys. 'Are you going too?'

'Yes,' said Betsi Wyn. 'Do you think the pirates will be friendly?'

Emyr Rhys shook his head. 'No,' he said. 'Pirates are fierce.'

'Well, I'm not going to be scared,' Betsi Wyn said. 'I've got a magic kiss. If I feel scared I just have to remember that *sws* and I'll be fine.' And she held up her hand to show Emyr Rhys.

'I can't see anything,' he said.

'That's because it's magic,' said Betsi Wyn.

As they got nearer to Gwion's house, Betsi Wyn and Emyr Rhys could see a big black pirate flag tied to the gate. They could hear lots of shouting and they could see pirates chasing each other round and round the garden.

Emyr Rhys stopped. 'The pirates look very fierce,' he said. 'I wish I had a magic kiss like yours.'

Betsi Wyn thought for a moment. 'Here, Emyr Rhys,' she said. 'I've got two magic kisses. Hold my hand and you can have one of them.' And she held out her hand.

Emyr Rhys didn't want to hold Betsi Wyn's hand, not with everyone watching. But they were getting very close to Gwion's garden. The pirates looked bigger now and their shouts were even louder.

Suddenly Emyr Rhys grabbed Betsi Wyn's hand. 'Thanks,' he said. 'I'll remember that magic kiss if I get scared.'

But then he thought of something else.

'What if the kiss falls off my hand at the party and gets lost?'

'Oh no,' said Betsi Wyn solemnly, 'that magic kiss won't fall off or get lost. That kiss is stuck tight to your hand.'

Emyr Rhys smiled. 'That's good,' he said. He was feeling quite brave now. 'Come on, Betsi Wyn, let's go.'

They ran to the gate and Gwion opened it. He was wearing a black eyepatch. 'Come aboard, me hearties,' he said in a piratey voice. 'There be treasure in this garden. Ooh arr!'

Gwion's black eyepatch was funny. And so was his piratey voice. Betsi Wyn and Emyr Rhys began to laugh.

'Thanks for sharing the magic kiss, Betsi Wyn,' Emyr Rhys said. 'I think these pirates are friendly after all.' He held up his thumb to Da-cu.

'I think so too,' said Betsi Wyn. 'Look!' She pointed at two pirates who were holding up shiny golden coins. 'There's Carys and Anwen.'

'We're hunting for treasure,' Anwen called. 'Chocolate pennies. Come and help us.'

Betsi Wyn turned to Mam-gu with a smile. 'I'm going to like this party,' she said. 'Bye, Mam-gu. See you later.'

And Betsi Wyn ran off with Emyr Rhys, Carys, Anwen and all the other pirates to hunt for hidden chocolate treasure.

'Ooh arr!'

About the Author

As a child growing up in Llanelli, I loved spending time in the local library. On Saturday afternoons I'd browse the shelves, searching for books to borrow and lose myself in. When I was older, I was fortunate enough to work in that same library. It was amazing to be surrounded by so many books on so many different subjects. Later, when I was a primary school teacher, I enjoyed sharing my favourite stories with the children in my class. And they shared their favourites with me. We made up our own tales too.

I still live in west Wales, with my husband and children, and I still love books and making up stories. I hope you enjoy reading about Betsi Wyn and Emyr Rhys. It was great fun writing about them.

Wendy White